TRANSPORTED

TALES OF MISFORTUNE & ROGUERY

———

Written & illustrated by

BRIAN HARRISON-LEVER

Launceston, Tasmania
2017

———

DEDICATION

To the people of Van Diemen's Land.
May we treasure and protect our beautiful island, remembering and
giving thanks to those here before us, of all colours, castes and creeds.

—Brian Harrison-Lever

INTRODUCTION

Wars generate wealth for some and employment for many; when peace is declared, one-time thriving industries close down, resulting in depressed labour markets. The Napoleonic wars were no exception. After Waterloo in 1815, Britain's towns and countryside were awash with demobilised military veterans, unemployed weapons-makers, shipyard workers, seamstresses, tailors, weavers and farm workers. As social welfare was practically non-existent, crime flourished.

For a while the overcrowding of British jails was a 'dilemma', solved, authorities considered, with 'prison hulks' — the rotting remnants of Nelson's battle fleet. This was only ever to be a temporary solution, a holding area often for the unfortunates destined for Transportation. Between the years 1788 and 1868, men, women and children branded 'felons' were shipped to the penal colonies of the Australian mainland and Van Diemen's Land, often for offences that in today's world would be considered little more than petty crimes.

What happened to those fortunates who survived the long, perilous voyage is generally well documented; we know their names, ages, and crimes. We can discover how their lives panned out during the many

INTRODUCTION

years of assignment and hard labour, and what befell them once they earned their tickets of leave. We know very little, however, of who they were as human beings before conviction. Research of the archives allows one to dig a little deeper into some lives before transportation, particularly with the more renowned — the political prisoners for example, and some of the notorious villains who escaped the hangman's noose. Of the previous lives of the lesser known cases, the majority, we can only speculate.

The following little narratives told in rhyme make no pretence at being factual accounts of real people. Rather, they are an attempt to shine a light through and beyond the bland fog of statistics to what might have been the previous lives and reasons for transgressions of people who were transported.

Rhyme, I believe, is easy to read and allows a lot of ground to be covered in a few short lines. If written with a simple rhythm, like folk-song lyrics, the words and (in this case) the fictional people they briefly bring to life, may prompt the reader's imagination to travel a little beyond the numerical data of dry, historical records. This is my intention.

—Brian Harrison-Lever
Launceston, Tasmania
June 2016

PROLOGUE

There was a time when 'British justice' was a blatant contradiction,
Just a catch-all phrase the privileged used to gain a quick conviction.
As a consequence the prisons, jails and lock-ups were congested
With the nation's poor, its criminals and those the rich detested.

How to ease this situation was a question much debated,
And the costs involved in feeding them could not be understated!
The ruling classes scratched their heads and mused in pure vexation,
We have to find alternatives — perhaps beyond this nation?

We've colonies across the seas demanding more support.
The answer to their calls for help is standing in this court!
So that's how transportation of convicted felons started,
Leaving many families destitute, alone and broken hearted.

Conditions on the early fleets, degrading and deprived,
Had convicted felons live in filth, and very few survived.
In later years provisos changed and onus was conceded
A living healthy labour force was what the outposts needed.

Ship's surgeons made inspections then, and hygiene was advanced,
All rations, clothing, exercise, would have to be enhanced.
Despite improved confinement-cells and crowding less severe,
Five months on a transport ship was dreadful, let's be clear.

For fifty years the British packed their 'problems' into ships
And sent them half around the world on less than pleasure trips.
The down-and-out, the dissidents, and gentry on hard times,
Were bundled in with brutal types who boasted of their crimes.

For some it was a journey over Dante's River Styx,
And others — well, one must concede they suffered in the mix.
The journey's end was welcomed by both convicts and the crews —
Though a future in Van Diemen's Land was hardly one they'd choose.

Now, who were these unfortunates condemned to servitude:
Noose-candidates, life's reprobates, the fearful and the rude,
Homeless children lacking learning and sad villains in despair,
Such a mix of Britain's rejects who had lost the will to care?

On felon's names and vessel tonnage we find modest dereliction,
But there's very little narrative of lives before conviction.
So let us muse upon those times when righteous, bald hypocrisy
Was used against 'the rights of man' by church and aristocracy.

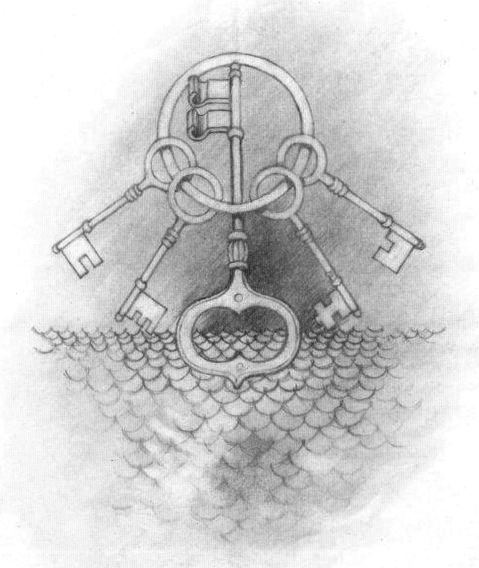

DRAMATIS PERSONAE

HON. FREDERICK BONNINGTON-HAUGH

Old Bailey Judge

My day was quite oppressive: far too many in the dock.

How, one wonders, can one manage? Then one's feelings run amok.

Patience rattled by these cases, so much 'pleading' one can take.

Limits passed before the noon-time when the court must take a break.

Stifling heat and stench abhorrent — how these sessions test my strength.

No acceptance, less repentance, plaintive whimpering tales at length.

Is there no respect for status? Don't these villains know their place?

Most speak gibberish, hardly English, so much 'tosh' — a damned disgrace!

In amongst these social misfits stood a 'petite bourgeoisie'.

He had breeding, education — and a problem, one could see!

Several days of Newgate pampering had played havoc with his style,

Last week's shirt could do with changing — that'll have to wait a while.

Prosecution's case convincing: this young bounder's stolen cash.
Lived a life above his stipend, forging banknotes. Now, that's rash!
Credit letters, deeds and titles — been quite handy with a pen,
Paying debts with 'non-such money'. Well, he won't do that again!

Then milady from the laundry claims she 'didn't mean no 'arm' —
Helped herself to half a wardrobe, tried to win me with her charm.
A little brat who knew no better lifting kerchiefs from the best,
Snotty nose and crafty fingers — well, I'm sure you know the rest.

On they went, these sorry stories — 'No I didn't, wasn't me',
'Tripped 'n' fell, 'e did, yer honner, banged 'is nose against my knee'.
Worst of all a flashy veteran wearing clothes he'd likely thieved,
Charged with beating, theft and menace — to be seen to be believed!

Courtroom crowded: gawps and riff-raff, tears and jeers and ribald laughter,
Should have hired a troupe of singers — circus clowns is what they're after.
Drury Lane's less entertaining. Pantomime could not compare.
'Bring refreshments, feed the famished' — Lift my wig and tear my hair!

Black-robed clerks and legal whatnots, sniggering, snuffling, shuffling papers.
Seen the lot, these 'cultured toffees', not impressed with felons' capers.
Not much interest in my summaries, more impressed with peer group natter,
'Learned friends!' An oxymoron! Yawning, fawning — does it matter?

Where to go with formal utterance, what pronouncement should one make?
Not my place to be subjective. 'Clear the Court, for heaven's sake.'
Washed my hands of rational judgments, just ignored defendants' pleas.
No room left in England's prisons? 'Transportation overseas!'

BARNABY HEATH

Shepherd, Age 28

Each morning as the cockerels crowed we'd walk familiar tracks,
My grazing 'charges' all about, mist-droplets on their backs.
Black Bobby trotted at my heels, his foggy breath a measure
Of the early hour and frosty air that gave me so much pleasure.

My Meg and I first met and kissed on May Day on the green.
The Morris Dancers jigged and sang and banged their tambourine
While children laughed and danced around the maypole in the middle.
Old Charlie from the Rose and Crown, he played his two-stringed fiddle.

Her father, he encouraged me: he'd several unwed daughters.
The shepherd's job it came to me with comfy married quarters.
An early morn, a hill-top dawn, the woolly smell of wethers,
A blackbird's song, a rising lark, the gorse-bush and the heathers.

We married at the local church. Sweet Meg, she looked so pretty.
For ten good years we had it all — I spoiled it more's the pity!
My shepherd's life, my kids, my wife, you'd think I didn't care.
I swear I'd never steal again if I could get back there.

My troubles started at the inn when lambing time was done.
I'd several ewes delivered twins — more profit than just one!
My farmer hadn't counted up; he'd been off in the city,
The boozers offered cash for lambs — I took it more's the pity!

Old Silas was the farmer then, his eyesight gave him trouble.
When counting up his Suffolk stock I'd tell him he'd seen double.
'Well count 'em for me son,' he'd say, 'you know I'd trust your ruling.'
'Twas easy then to keep the score, despite I'd had no schooling.

A Cotswolds village market day; and gossip my undoing,

My farmer might be 'getting on', but stories had him stewing:

His shepherd boy was selling stock and pocketing the lolly!

He had me hauled before the Wig, who charged me with my folly.

No pleas of debt, dependent wife, or children helped my case.

My family, they appeared in court to witness my disgrace.

Six months in a prison hulk on mud-flats half afloat,

Then transportation 'round the world on board a convict boat.

They moved us then, four score and ten, some thieves and rogues and debtors.

We clanked aboard our transport ship a troop of lags in fetters.

The crew they grinned and scrubbed us down; they didn't seemed to care,

We've months to go now down below now — sailing, God knows where?

Shepherd's Wife, Age 24

Convicted! Oh no, not my husband my man.
I've prayed for acquittal since this trial began.
Please, my lords, in your mercy don't take him away,
He has children to care for, what more can I say?

There's no case against him! Is something amiss?
How could you convict him — what justice is this?
His crime was an act of unthinking deceit,
A fault that in hindsight he'd never repeat.

He's a good man, my Barney, a fool not a thief.
A father, a worker — there's worth underneath.
How on earth will we manage with no man to care?
Don't break up our family — My God! I despair!

We've three little children and nowhere to rest.
There's Mattie and Rosie and Nell at my breast.
With winter approaching, our home, dispossessed,
We'll beg by the roadside, and starve there at best.

They are turning their backs on my pleading and tears,
Their lordships so haughty confirming my fears.
A sentence so wicked, we're crippled with grief —
Seven years transportation! It beggars belief!

He'll be gone in the morning, my husband, my mate,
My children's proud father — my pleas are too late.
In cold desperation, my prayers now in tatters,
I cling to my children. They're all now that matters.

I've lost him, my darling, they'll take him away
To the end of the earth now, I've heard people say.
Chained up and transported, deprived of all hope,
He'll be sick with the worry of how we will cope.

Must put on a brave face and say my goodbyes,
Hold his hand for a minute. We both realise
This moment in time that we now have to face
Is the last chance we'll have for a fleeting embrace.

Ushered out of the door into Bailey's drab street,
Just the clothes on my back and the weans at my feet.
Take a man from his family and what happens then,
With no help for the homeless? A heartless 'Amen'.

JACOB ENTWHISTLE

Weaver, Age 30

My dad had been a weaver — all his life he'd kicked the pedal,
As my grandpa did before 'im; both men worked the hand-loom treadle.
From the age of nearly seven I had watched and learned the trade,
Used my hands to load the shuttle for the worsted that we made.

Canny lads those cottage workers how they managed woollen weft,
Interlacing threads for textiles, throwing shuttles right and left.
Hats were raised to village weavers in those days of family pride;
There was money in the trade then, and a few days off beside.

Then the gentry from the big house opened up the Blackstone Mill.
Fifty looms all powered by water — would they need their weavers still?
Fifty times the daily output from these monster, clacking looms,
Less than half the workers needed — much more profit, one assumes!

Wages dropped and work hours lifted. Twelve hours standing on your feet,
Stagger home to wife and children — where there's little left to eat.
Can't go on, but no one listening when we plead for living wages,
Only interest is their profit — best the owners made for ages!

Rue the day those smart inventors when they played with water power,
Then came up with steam-pushed shuttles, making cottage work turn sour.
Gone the times of home-wove worsted, absent now the weaver's pride.
Towering chimneys, smoke filled skylines — simple men just weep inside.

'Discontent will lead to trouble,' Vicar pleads, but action's praised.
Gathering storm from unemployment, threats ignored and banners raised,
Luddite meetings, voices screaming. Can't we stop this exploitation?
Smash the power looms! March on London! Save our families from starvation!

'Read the Riot Act — call the guards out,' yelled the top-hats in their fright.
Flash of sabres, horses stamping, red-coat troopers — that's not right!
No-one wanted broken bones or blood-stained chapters to this tale:
Weeping widows, orphaned children, sons and husbands locked in jail.

Four and twenty charged with treason. 'Hang the lot!' the bosses shouted.
Cries of outrage, calls for reason, women bashed and children clouted.
Show-trial justice for the weavers — little hope once gavel banged.
Most were sentenced, some transported, few released — and others hanged.

Smashing looms made little difference; those that broke 'em suffered more:
Transportation for the many to Van Diemen's distant shore.
Now I listen in the darkness of this ocean-battered cell
For the cry of 'Land in sight there!' just to know that all is well.

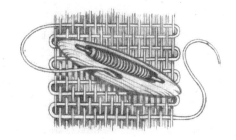

ARNOLD CLOBBER

Footpad, Age 33

Twelve years in the infantry I fought at Waterloo,

End up with nowt, we're most kicked out; they only kept a few.

'No one wants a soldier when there's no threat at the door':

Seems to me I'm thinking that I've heard that song before.

When we were marching over Europe making village church-bells ring,

Many made big juicy profits selling victuals to the King.

Guns and drums and yokels by the thousand needed then,

When the fighting is all over — 'You can all go home again.'

Three of us we walked to town old uniforms and leather.

Our coats had holes, boots missing soles, we opt to stick together.

How to earn a living when the 'Old Duke's' war was won?

Just as well we're singles as a family wouldn't be fun.

Lots of chubby drinkers in the Inns on Friday night.
Three of us could drop one, lift his purse — it's only right:
Probably made his shillings out of wartime tack and such,
Buy us beer and porky sausage, should be such an easy touch.

So that's how we got started, knocking tipsy revellers flat,
Lifting rings and things and clothing — got mi-self a flashy hat!
Over time we dressed quite smartly and the ladies made a note,
Of me fancy doeskin britches and me 'mind-your-manners' coat.

We were gaining reputation as a crafty, nasty crew,
Other veterans getting mindful of the things we chose to do,
Like flooring helpless drunkards with a spot of fist and boot,
And the cash that we were making by just picking up the loot.
For several years we stoked the fears of travellers after dark

At Primrose Brow and Hampstead Row, then down in Regents Park.
Though Bow Street Runners kept a watch for villains as demanded,
'The three bright lads' 'revered Footpads', we left 'em empty handed.

They laid a trap, the Runners did to 'catch him whilst he's sleeping'.
The other two had long shot through — the loot was in their keeping.
'You're done for, Arnold! Goose is cooked! They'll string you up like mutton!
Get dressed, old son, your times begun; here's convict irons to put on.'

In Bow Street dock the Judge takes stock of a soldier's life reputed.
Expecting death, I gasp for breath — my sentence is commuted!
'Van Diemen's Land will suit him grand; they need tough veteran labour,
When his ship docks he'll break up rocks whilst chained up to his neighbour.'

NATHANIEL BATES

Forger, Age 22

With education, family name, nd writing skills aplenty,
The city flesh-pots, drink and such, appealed at two and twenty.
My cash allowance seemed enough, so 'why get into debt?'
My father's questions haunt me still — his words I'll not forget.

Now making money isn't hard, they told me at the club,
But knowing how to make enough — it's tricky! That's the rub.
There is a way with cash today requires a steady nerve,
I know I must break father's trust to get what I deserve.

A pot of ink, a fresh trimmed quill, and half an hour of cheating,
Three five-pound notes, the ink still wet, set my young heart a-beating.
The first two, dodgy, blots and all would never fool a teller.
The third attempt — as good as gold! — deceived my tailor fellah.

My talent found, my future sound, my forging hand succeeding,
Why think of ill when sharpened quill provides for all I'm needing?
My reputation round the town for settling debts outstanding,
And spending money right and left had creditors demanding.

From five pound notes to fifty pounds, my skills were getting better.
Conceit and over confidence ... I forged a credit letter!
My father tried to save my skin: he'd pay out all my debts.
The Bow Street Runner shook his head and offered his regrets.

My cultured voice and pedigree did nothing for my case.
His honour with a scornful tone remarked of my disgrace,
'Your conduct and your actions, sir, leave much to be desired,
The sentence is appropriate.' With that, the judge retired.

Transportation, fourteen years! It broke my father's heart.
A Newgate cell, a life of hell before the ships depart.
He came to see me every day, he wrote so many letters,
My life was ruined — as was his, deserted by his betters.

On Plymouth wharf we wave goodbye, no chance for last embrace.
'Felons all, respond to call!' We're soldier marched apace.
Forgers, poachers, tarts and thieves all board the ship 'Renown',
There's hatches opened, ladders steep, and convicts bundled down.

Shanties singing, ships bells ringing, calls to haul on ropes,
Plymouth town now slides astern and with it all our hopes.
'Van Diemen's Land is months away.' — at least that's what we're told.
Meanwhile we squat, and fret, and wait, inside this stinking hold.

POPPY WORKHOUSE

Flower Girl, Age 12

Little Poppy Workhouse was very fond of flowers.

She'd sleep beneath a hawthorn hedge then search the woods for hours:

A bluebell and a lilac bloom, a buttercup or two

Would make a pretty posy; she only took a few.

Her gypsy life was kind in June, in winter less forgiving.

No matter how the seasons changed, she had to earn a living.

A coronet of daisies might fetch a crust of bread?

Or sing a song of marigolds and earn some, coins instead?

At Spaniards Inn on summer nights, young blades most smartly dressed

Would bow and flirt each pretty skirt; the ladies were impressed.

'Your name, I pray, my lucky day, the gods have smiled upon it,

You look divine! A glass of wine? Some flowers for your bonnet?'

He'd look around and, Poppy found, would buy a little spray.
'Now hop it smart, you little tart,' was all he'd have to say.
Poor little child. Some patrons smiled, and others bought her blooms.
With smarting feet and naught to eat she'd wander through the rooms.

Wild flowers grow on Hampstead Heath. The seasons come and go.
Bleak autumn and there's little left, as any child would know.
Selling flowers on London's streets was not a misdemeanour,
She picked a few from Regents Park — and someone must have seen her!

She'd stolen flowers; she'd begged for food; she'd managed as did many.
'What family has this child?' They asked. — 'Well, sirs, she hasn't any!'
Abandoned at the age of ten, in London's crime-filled city,
She'd lived out rough and stolen stuff. They caught her, more's the pity.

The magistrate, he scratched his wig. What choices were on hand?
She needed food, a roof and such, they had to understand.
To turn her out on London's streets, a life of crime and graft,
Or send her to Van Diemen's Land aboard a transport craft?

'Seven years transportation, she'll learn a skill or two —
A parlour maid could be her trade; she'll start her life anew.
These felons given half a chance, and half is all we're giving,
In Hobart town can serve their time then earn an honest living.'

So Poppy sailed with many more from Plymouth in September.
Conditions on the trip were tough, a cruise they'd all remember.
Five long months through storm and calm, through sickness and privation,
Our flower girl, she survived the trip, and helped to build a nation.

SAM CROPPER

Poacher, Age 33

On a sharp winter's eve with a northerly chill,
I'd set rabbit snares in the copse on a hill.
His Lordship's estate was a favourite trick,
But you had to be knowing, light-fingered and quick.

Old eagle-eyed Bagshaw, his Lordship's gamekeeper,
Was fast on his feet but he was a sound-sleeper.
He'd seldom step out on a cold winter's night
When there's frost on the heath and a breeze with a bite;

Any squeal from the thickets he wouldn't get nosy —
With a fire in the hearth, his thatched cottage was cosy.
He'd shut up the shutters and just shake his head,
Blow out the candle, and climb into bed.

Now rabbits is one thing, and not without hope,
But a brace of prize pheasants could get you the rope!
The Earl loved his shooting, his birds and his deer,
He'd pot-shot at poachers for pheasants, no fear!

Feeding six kids on a farm-hand's poor pay
Can be done if you're thrifty, the gentlefolk say.
Now, thrifty is one thing; but what can you do
When their shoes and their clothing are all but worn through?

When the shelves in the cupboard are empty and bare
Not a mouse or a cockroach would feed well in there.
We needed some pennies for victuals and cloth,
So I gambled old Bagshaw would take a night off.

Game-birds will sell in the market for cash,
But poaching fat pheasants would have to be rash.
They caught me, the watchmen, the birds in my pack.
His Lordship said, 'Flog him! Put stripes on his back!'

In the dock it was 'guilty', and no use denying.
My wife and the young-uns were pleading and crying.
The judge so bad tempered, impassive, prevailing,
Snapped, 'Take this rogue down, and enough of this wailing.'

'Then tickle his back with the lash a few times,
And that isn't all that he'll get for his crimes:
A cruise on a transport and seven years in fetters,
Will teach this farm lout not to steal from his betters.'

BETTY DUSTER

Chamber Maid, Age 16

Up at dawning every morning, seven plodding days a week,
Carry coals up, light the fires. I get weary, so to speak.
Madam this and madam that, and 'curtsy when you meet her,'
'Grubby hands girl, fix your hair now.' 'Apron could be neater!'

Footmen, maids and kitchen staff in line and 'Stand up straight!'
Laboured breathing, Butler seething, breakfast can't be late!
'Times are hard and choices few.' His lecture never varies.
Bleary eyed and half awake, my mind's off with the fairies!

Days in service, nights in dreaming of a better, happy life —
Some rich farmer loves me dearly, takes me with him for his wife.
Life goes on and nothing changes, polish, clean and dust all day.
Family needs my monthly shillings — nothing more that I can say.

'Lead us not into temptation, thank the Lord for roof and bread.'
Is it wrong to envy riches and to yearn for more instead?
Madam's dresser, pretty trinkets, broaches rings, perfumes and such —
All need dusting, Madam trusting that her chamber-maid won't touch.

Enticing glitter is corrupting when confronted with such treasure.
There were toiletries and knick-knacks just to try on at my leisure.
Such a foolish lapse in reason, why I thought no-one would guess.
'Did you take the silver hair-brush?' — 'Yes I did, I must confess.'

'You've shamed us all.' My parents tell me, they were glad to see me go.
Seek another job in service — not much point; the answer's 'NO!'
There's no help for one so tarnished, reputation torn to shreds,
Walk the roads and beg for pennies, or the poorhouse-roof one dreads.

Destitute, so cold and hungry — steal some little things to sell,
Lift a loaf from baker's barrow ... and his money purse as well!
Can't run fast in worn-out slippers when the cobblestones are wet—
Grabbed my hair, this floury fat man — language foul. He was upset.

The magistrate was most unpleasant: 'Silence, wench, there's no excuse!
Your name we know and reputation. Stand up straight, to beg's no use.
Milady's hairbrush, cash and foodstuff, now you ask for amnesty?
Wait your time in Newgate Prison, few weeks there and then we'll see.'

That dreadful man! His time for thinking didn't last a day or three.
Hauled me up to hear my sentence: 'Hangman's Noose ... or ... let me see ...'
Plymouth docks and board a transport, fourteen years to contemplate.
Never thought I'd end up travelling, better that than t'other fate.

TICKER TOFF

Petty Thief, Age 17

Lifting watches was my game. I had a sound repute.

My standing in the ticker trade was one without dispute.

There's likely lads could nick and run, but none had my finesse:

Just place your order, name your brand, it's yours and no distress.

I took my chances early on, but practice leads to knowledge:

No point in thinking half a crown when tapping Eton College,

Gents who dress with valet touch and carry gold-topped canes,

Have pretty Hunters' on their fobs, and breeding in their veins.

London taverns Friday nights attract the fashion dandies.

There's flighty ladies' winks and nods for those who have the handies.

A quaff or two of local brew, then fathers' warnings vanished,

She's less than fair, but should he care? — All prudent judgement banished.

Two tanners buy the best Havanas' — hour or two of drinking.
Ladies giggly, gents quite tiddly — make my move, I'm thinking.
Waiter's apron, look the part: 'Those glasses, sir, I'll clear 'em,'
Push and shoving crowded bar-room helps to get me near 'em.

Towel concealing crafty fingers probing rich brocade,
Lift the ticker, couldn't be quicker, best the Swiss have made!
Find the door and ease out slowly not to raise mistrust,
Cross the cobbles through the stables, hide there if I must.

The 'Ticker Toff' I'm known as local: envy there, and spite,
Silver-buttoned velvet jacket — 'ties his stock just right!' —
'Never seen a lad from Finchley don such airs and graces!'
Jealousy's a problem for me — seen it in their faces.

Done me down, that tavern doxy, sold me for a quid.
Told the traps where I'd be hiding — gave her tips, I did!
'Gotcha, Ticker, caught red handed, goods still in yer pocket!'
Down the lock-up, slam the door — they don't forget to lock it!

Newgate Prison's not the place I thought I'd ever visit.
Not the little Ticker Shop I'd set my heart on, is it?
What went wrong? I ask myself, how did I end up busted?
That fickle biddy soaked in gin I should've never trusted.

In the dock before the Beak, I plead for understanding.
Seven years' transportation is what the law's demanding.
Time's my trade and time's my sentence, ages 'til I'm free!
Locked in hold of convict transport heading out to sea.

JANE POUNCER

Laundry Maid, Age 18

A paisley shawl was my downfall. I should have known much better.
'Forgive me Marm, I meant no harm. Please write a reference letter.'
'No letter, Jane. I'll make it plain: you've gone too far this time,
They'll lock you up; that's your bad luck; you'll pay the price for crime.

My paisley shawl ... but that's not all! I know you've taken bread!
You'll get seven years, no use for tears, so pack your bag instead.'
'I only took a loaf or two! There's plenty in the larder!'
'That's no excuse!' She screamed abuse. 'You're going to make things harder!'

The Master called the guard at once and held me 'til they came.
'She's just a little laundry scrub, Jane Pouncer is her name.'
'Take her away,' —I heard him say, 'Ignore her plea for pity.'
The soldiers joked and pinched and poked, and dragged me to the city.

The Magistrate, he came in late. We'd waited round the clock.
My dirty dress — I looked a mess there, weeping in the dock.
'What say you maid? This court's delayed, we haven't time for crying.'
I couldn't speak, my legs felt weak. He'd know if I was lying.

His icy stare, he couldn't care, compassion quite bereft.
'Two years,' he said 'for taking bread, another five for theft.
Transport her south — and shut her mouth, I will not have this wailing.
A Newgate cell will suit her well until it's time for sailing.'

A month went by. No sun, no sky. Just straw and stone and wet.
The warders cruel, the food cold gruel, despair that's with me yet.
Then, blessed day! They came to say 'We're moving you to Devon.'
An open cart! We'd made a start. To breathe fresh air was heaven.

Off we trundled, bound and bundled; oh what degradation.
Bumpy tracks we can't relax. The coast our destination.
Plymouth nearing, locals cheering, hide our heads in shame.
'You're not the first or near the worst,' I heard the crowd exclaim.

There's masts and spars, Marines and tars, and hubbub round the town,
Our pleas ignored, we're pressed on board the transport ship 'Renown'.
'She's light and tight and ship-shape bright; her crew are tough,' we're told.
We don't see much, just ropes and such — then prodded down the hold.

The voyage bleak, so I won't speak of sickness and despairing.
A hundred, though, were locked below the decks with no-one caring.
We land at last, our ordeal past; there's sunshine and blue sky.
So come what may I'll hope and pray we'll prosper bye and bye.

WILLIAM DANCER

Highwayman, Age 25

Since childhood on a rural farm excitement's been my mentor.
Young Jenny from the Shipyard Inn, I thought that fate had sent her.
This lovely girl who served the grog and teased me with her charms
Suggested we could make a pair and work the roads and farms.

A mounted duo riding hard with pistols, masks and curses
Could halt the mail-coach, threaten death, and take the cash-filled purses,
Then canter off across the heath with small chance of pursuit
Each time avoiding well used paths; we'd choose a different route.

In manly clothes and hidden face she fooled our frightened prey.
Two highway-'men' worked very well, and fortune smiled our way.
We sought the roads where riches went and hunted down the coaches.
Our victims, wealthy businessmen, yelled after us reproaches!

We were a couple worked the roads when others sought their beds,
Well mounted and our pistols primed, with prices on our heads.
There comes a time in any crime when loyalty is needed,
My lovely partner let me down. The red-coats' hooves she heeded.

She left my side and cantered off before I knew the reason.
Some other watchful highway thief would shout before such treason.
They rode me down and bailed me up. I had no chance, not then.
My lovely lass, she disappeared. I'll not see her again.

Newgate slops and rusting bars have been my fate a year now.
Foolish was the last mad trick that lead my fate to here now.
Fourteen years they handed down: transported, bound in chains,
For holding up the midnight coach, hard labour for my pains!

Sweating timber, heaving deck, fetid air to breath now,
In crowded hold of prison barque old England's shores we leave now.
Once I dressed in fashion cloth with boots of Spanish leather.
Once I rode an Arab mare through open fields and heather.

Sweet Jenny waved our ship away. I wonder what she'll do?
Before we've past the harbour mouth she'll earn a coin or two.
No grieving lass to weep and moan — but who could ever blame her?
They asked who rode the second mount: she knew I'd never name her.

My fate is set, my future grim. No point in useless tears.
Van Diemen's Land without a doubt will live up to my fears.
So Jenny, sweet goodbye; good luck. I'll learn from my mistake.
Don't let your next man down like me ... shout out, for goodness sake!

ELIZA PLEAT

Seamstress, Age 23

Threading needles in poor light will play bad tricks upon one's sight,
And after dusk the candle's flame will flicker.
With milady's maid complaining and near thirteen years eye-straining,
A poor seamstress has a problem working quicker.

There were always several orders, many pin-tucks and braid borders,
Hidden seams on yards and yards of silk brocade.
Tiny buttonholes and such, making fingers sore to touch,
Much hard work on all those dresses that we made.

With so many make-and-mends, work all hours the good Lord sends.
It's no wonder a poor girl could not see straight.
When the ball-gown wasn't finished, reputation quite diminished,
My position in the household's in debate.

Where to go? My brain is wracking. If milady sends me packing,
How to manage when my wages are no more?
So much fabric for the taking, bought for dresses we're not making —
Silks and satins, threads and ribbons here galore.

One could blame fatigue and worry for decisions in a hurry,
Opportunity was staring in my face.
Quite a dozen yards of satin with a modish, floral pattern,
And a bolt of Flanders' famous bobbin lace.

So, your honour, I confess to a crime whilst in distress.
Now I place myself before the court in shame.
I must plead for understanding — not the fate the law's demanding —
Just a chance to make amends and clear my name.

The Magistrate looked angry; he'd clearly had enough.
All morning he'd been listening to the same depressing stuff.
His luncheon it was waiting in the chambers, he'd been told,
He wasn't really listening as his soup was getting cold!

'Eliza Pleat stop this deceiving, your crime is wilful thieving,
An example must be made this very day.
You will leave this honest nation for a spell of transportation:
Seven years of laundry scrubbing, I would say.'

So I found myself escorted to a ship and then deported
With a hundred other felons — oh, the shame!
We are heading God knows where. Will we get there? I don't care.
I have only got my silly self to blame.

STANLEY SMOGG

Pick Pocket, Age 12

The city streets had been my home, I never had a proper,

I'd fed myself and everyfing and never come a cropper.

They taught me fings, the streets they did, they made me very clever,

Like how to nick a bob or two then beat-it hell-for-leather.

I was the lad. I knew the trade of lifting pocket flaps —

That was, until I messed things up and tried it on the traps.

They chased me down in old Brick Lane and caught me. 'What's the use?'

Though twelve years old and orphaned too, I'm told, 'That's no excuse!'

They cuffed my ears and bound my hands and dragged me off to jail.

I screamed and scratched and kicked and spat, but all to no avail.

The beak, he give me seven long years 'transported' for my sins —

Tomorrow morning, rain or blow, my sea-born life begins.

TRANSPORTED

Once aboard the transport ship, I take a look about.

'Get down that ladder all of you!' I hear the sergeant shout.

There's villains here, a nasty lot, and ruffians galore

In chains and shame. There's gentry too! I've not seen that before.

Just days ago I'd scrounge and steal to get a crust of bread.

On board this ship its tacky-stew they're handing out instead!

One blanket each, a pair of boots, warm britches and a vest,

A jacket too, that's not worn through! I'll keep this one for best!

I never used to wash mi self, I never cut mi hair,

But now I'm scrubbed and clipped and such, that give me quite a scare!

There's lads like me crammed down this hold, our faces getting paler,

Young convicts in a wave-tossed box — who'd want be a sailor?

The guards they keep an eye on us. No mixing with the men,
No getting out of line down here or feel the boot again.
Just frightened kids, the youngest ones; some cry for home and mother.
Well, not much point in fretting now — at least we've got each other.

The voyage long, the weather foul, the vomit and the poo,
Hard slams the ocean 'cross our bows. 'This boat will split in two!'
The youngsters wail, the posh ones pray, the rest just curse and roar.
The crew they haul and shorten sail, they've seen it all before.

One morning as the eight bells ring, the blow has passed us by.
We felons now can mount the steps and see the blessed sky!
There's Hobart Town across the bay and soldiers there to greet us,
My future's here for seven long years. I wonder how they'll treat us.

JOSEPH MUGGINS

Footman, Age 18

Apprentice footman waiting-on beside His Lordship's table
And moving up the ranks I'd be, as soon as I was able.
In service in a 'stately home'. It didn't come by chance:
My uncle worked the estate farm and helped me to advance.

'Don't speak until you're spoken to, and clear away the dishes.
For other chores you open doors and tend to master's wishes.
The silver in the cutlery drawers is worth a pretty penny —
When cleaning it you don't use spit ... and don't go losing any!'

Well, that was several months ago, advice I should have heeded.
When laying out the cutlery I took more than I needed.
Temptation is the devil's work, that's what we learned in chapel:
'You break the rules you pay the price' — like Eve and Adam's apple.

'Seven years for borrowing stuff! I only meant to clean it!
I've polished silver oft enough, please sir, I didn't mean it.
Who said I tried to pinch these bits, who ever made such claim?
Please tell me sir, and let me have the villain's family name.'

My plea of lack of evidence was greeted with much laughter.
'You know, you rogue, it seems to me it's fourteen years you're after.
Take him down and box his ears. I've never heard such cheek!'
And that was really all there was. He wouldn't let me speak.

They dragged me down the cold stone steps and locked me in a cell.
The others there were ugly types and gentlemen as well!
Barred doors rattling, jail-mates prattling, little chance of sleeping,
Despair and dread, then shock instead to witness grown men weeping.

A month dragged by, then soldiers came to take us to the port.
We looked a troop of scruffy louts compared with our escort.
Four weeks filth and fed on slops, our ankles clad in chains,
His Lordship's footman smartly dressed — not much of him remains.

So here I am with rogues and cheats aboard a transport ship.
Best thing now is cope somehow, stay sweet throughout the trip.
No point making trouble as there's nothing there but sorrow,
Toe-the-line and I'll be fine ... another day tomorrow?

Down in the hold its freezing cold, it's crowded and it's wet.
The crew and soldiers up on deck are comfortable, I'll bet.
If I could swap with those up top I'd grab it in a trice,
Steal his Lordship's silver spoons? — Not worth it, my advice!

PATRICK DOHERTY

Irish Lawyer, Age 25

The blessed land with tear-washed skies, where hero Robert Emmet lies,
Now slips astern this pitching jail whilst Jack tars sing and haul up sail,
While redcoat soldiers stand at ease, the flapping topsails catch the breeze.
And down below this pretty play, one hundred felons rue the day.

One hundred men, their spirits down, their cause debunked before the crown,
Their pride mistreated, deeds decried. Emancipation hopes have died.
Some honest farmers pushed to breaking challenged laws not of their making.
Tenant croppers, desperate lives, presumed to challenge 'harvest tithes'!

The altercations, malcontent of laws that favoured Protestant.
Fat bishops, vicars, wealthy squires, and those constructing Gothic spires,
Scorn peasant-folk in rags and grief who looked to church for scant relief.
What this achieved was less than clear, with armed militia marching near.

Young hot-heads from the tenant mobs threw sticks then rocks at those with jobs.
These random acts of desperation echoed wide across the nation.
What once had been a plea to axe the pressures of a greedy tax
Became a call, a message stressed, a rally-cry for those oppressed,

With passion, fervour, wild elation: hopes for change, not confrontation.
Many came to add their voices, banners held demanding choices.
Others joined with low intent ... and anger now, their patience spent.
Discharging weapons, lives were lost! The tenant farmers bore the cost,

Their rights ignored. And was it a sin to start a fight they couldn't win?
So many hundreds went to trial, their cases had to wait a while.
A charge of treason, no defence — not one that offered any sense,
Not one that pardoned noncompliance, waywardness and armed defiance.

Though counselled not to get involved, determination quite resolved
My education, legal skills, must help me now to right these ills.
'Your Lordships hear my reasoning voice — these ill-used tenants had no choice.'
'We hear your voice and know your leaning. Those arguments have little meaning.'

From speaking out my die was cast — the time for stepping back was past.
Law-lords' verdicts elementary, hand in glove with church and gentry.
'Take them down and this man with them, treason proven, God forgive them.'
Stripped of status, bowed but brave, I joined the few I'd hoped to save.

One hundred Irish hanged that day and many more were sent away.
The 'many more', their faith in tatters, stripped of everything that matters,
Sent as exiles bound in chains to where no trace of hope remains —
Van Diemen's Land where this world ends — but British martial law attends.

JACK TAR

Seaman, Age 35

There's times when I get thinking that a life ashore would do,
When my days of salty mutton and a hammock bed are through,
But a month aground in Plymouth drinking witless sailor's joy
And a bit of rough and tumble with the local hoi—polloi?

Well, a seaman's wage it don't stretch far, but the grog makes him forget
All the climbing, hauling, bosun's bawling, days when he got wet.
After twenty years of ship-board it's a place to hide yer face
From the youngsters, screaming mothers, and the shore-bound human race!

Signing on the old tub's easy, and yer greeted like a friend.
It's the same old crew that's sailing, and it's mateship in the end.
'How's it going, Jack yer lubber, how's the fambly and the beer?
We could hug yer ugly mug, it's good to see yer, you old dear.'

Then there's weeks of paint and polish and a rope or two to splice;
Sluice the bilge out with the buckets, swabbing decks down once or twice.
Master's boarding in the morning, gotta have the crew look smart.
Get a shine on shoes and brasses; tarring pig-tales is an art!

When we've stowed the stores and victuals, got the hatches battened down
Then — a living line of misery shuffles our way from the town!
Jingling, clanking; soldiers flanking felons line the dock,
Such a sodden, bleating no retreating, scruffy convict flock.

Now a seaman's life ain't easy — just ask any tar you know —
But I'd rather climb a rat-line in a strong nor-wester blow
Than be shunted off to lord knows where in irons and disgrace,
With 'offender' written in mi book and tears upon mi face.

These wretches hardly human after six months tethered down
In a cell in Newgate Prison on the squalid side of town.
When we board 'em up the gangplank, there's a smell of rank despair,
Then we strip and scrub and clothe 'em. Now that's generous, to be fair.

When we've trimmed their matted locks off, and settled all the wailing,
They're shoved in the hold between-decks' while we rig the ship for sailing.
Time to turn your mind from misery, now the cargo's battened down,
And heed the bosun's yelling and the captain's worried frown.

Up the rat-lines to the yard arms, loose the mainsail, hang on fast!
One hand each for ship and sailor — now she's moving out at last.
Heading slow into the channel, bearing south, a friendly breeze,
Weather fair, we'll sail for months now — to the far Antipodes.

PRIVATE SMART

Marine, Age 20

'Twas the uniform that got me, bright red coat with braided lace,
Then the drum-roll at the market and the sergeant's cheery face:
'Make your mothers proud?' he shouted, 'Show 'em how you lads are willing!
All the girls'll love your outfits; take your King's enlistment shilling.

See the world and sail the oceans — there's no marching with a pack!
Lots of choices for promotion, maybe corporal down the track.
Easy life with no-one nagging, not so tough by any means,
Do your bit for king and country! Join King George's Royal Marines.'

Well, how's a lad to walk away in farmer-smock and clogs,
When a pint of beer and back-slaps landed him these flashy togs?
'Well, oi like the fancy clobber, where d'ya want mi sign mi cross?'
'You've joined up now, you bumpkin ... sergeant Barker is the boss!'

The next few weeks was tramp and swagger, boots are tight on blistered feet,
Trumpet calls and arms presented, uniforms must all look neat.
Rumour is we're bound for Plymouth, years and years we'll be away!
Off to war, or convict transport — sergeant's crafty, he won't say.

Once we start we know the answer: felon's escort if you please!
Six days marching down to Plymouth, then we travel overseas.
What a motley crew of prisoners, dressed in rags and chained together,
Shuffle on, no chance for resting, sleeping rough in any weather.

There she is, our destination, square-rigged transport ship 'Renown' —
Masts and spars and tarred-rope rigging, with her mainsails hanging down.
Blue-clad tars aloft and hauling, First Mate calling out, 'Belay!'
Stores and victuals on the dockside, and there's more to come, they say.

'Lobsters boarding!' shouts the bosun. All the Jack tars have a grin.
Not the greeting we expected. Sergeant takes it on the chin.
Our red tunics cause the laughter as we climb aboard the ship.
If it's teasing that we're after, then we'll get some on this trip.

One hundred convicts are our cargo, and they shuffle up the plank.
Captain reads the regulations as befits his lofty rank.
Once our moorings are all cast off and we're moving under sail
He's the one that gives the orders, and his rulings will prevail.

Red-coat 'lobsters' guard the convicts whilst the sailors do the rest.
It's the law on any transport, and the safest and the best.
Royal Marines are trained for fighting, not for hauling ropes in blocks
There's a role for each and all aboard until the vessel docks.

ROBERT MARINER

Captain, Age 39

'A LETTER HOME'

Goodbye, my dear wife, we will sail on the tide,
If fate had but blessed me you'd be by my side.
Our voyage this time will be long, I'm confessing,
And our cargo of felons you'd find most distressing.

I'm commissioned to transport these wretches away
To a land that will treat them more kindly, they say.
Our jails here are crowded, conditions outrageous,
Transportation is seen as a move advantageous.

Free settlers want labour to clear their new lands,
They need masons and tradesmen to work with their hands.
Their Lordships in wisdom conferred and agreed,
Transported young convicts should settle their need.

Conditions on board will be tight at the best.
We have less room than stables — they'll be most distressed.
When the weather is rough and there's sea down the hold
There'll be weeping and moaning and — riots, I'm told!

In the tropics for weeks when heat is intense,
Then resentment and rancour and fevers commence.
When the rations and water are low and infested,
Insurrection ensues, but it will be arrested.

Our Marines have their orders if things should get hot,
And our tars are all handy with powder and shot.
The bosun's a veteran. He's handled the worst —
A riot on this transport would not be his first.

With the threat of the lash and the look on his face
He'll not have much trouble with lags out of place.
We'll treat them as well as we can whilst at sea,
But they'll suffer and fret 'til the gods set them free.

The 'Renown' now: she's lively, and also our crew;
Our canvas, our rigging and timbers all new.
So our voyage, though long, and with risks now and then,
Will surely return us to Plymouth again.

So sweetheart don't worry, stay happy and bright.
I'll live for your news in the letters you write.
My safety's assured; and when I return
We'll purchase a home from the money I earn.

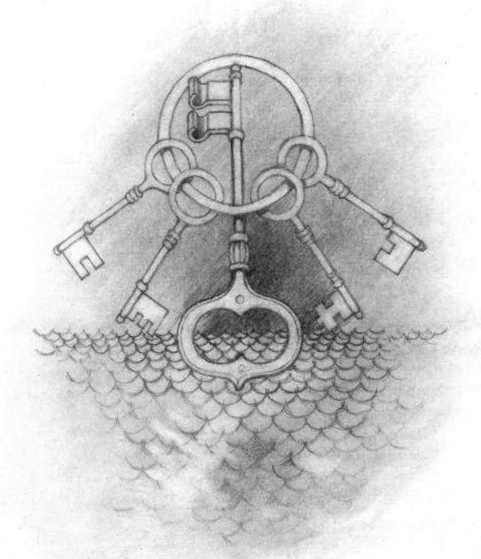

EPILOGUE

As the breeze filled the sails of the good ship 'Renown'
It was goodbye to Plymouth and sights of the town.
There were chores for the sailors. They climbed and they cleated;
A bosun's instruction was seldom repeated.

With the felons all fettered and holds battened fast,
Their long voyage south was beginning at last.
The cells they were crowded and tempers were frayed,
There were bullies who threatened and timid who prayed.

As the days became weeks and the ship struggled on,
All vestige of solace for the convicts was gone.
There was sickness from fevers and scurvy hit many.
Fresh fruit was an answer — there just wasn't any.

For the ailing and heartsick who longed to be free
The reprieve from rank suffering was burial at sea;
But most lived in hope that the ordeal would pass.
Weeks flowed into months as the sand in the glass.

Sweet breath from the forests and land birds in view
Brought relief to the captain and cheers from his crew.
'Land ho!' from the top-mast had the wretched rejoice.
Great delight was collective at the sound of that voice.

As 'Renown' docked in Hobart, salutes were exchanged.
Debarking male convicts was smartly arranged.
Some were snapped up for farm work and others, less suited,
Would labour on roads still in chains, it's reputed!

Of the women transported the skilful were taken;
The awkward, inept or 'with-child' were forsaken.
Some fortunate girls were assigned to good folk;
Others worked in the factories where life was no joke.

Times would always be hard for the worst reoffenders,
The unfortunate, luck-less Port Arthur contenders.
For those who chose tolerance and proffered repentance,
Hard work and compliance took time off their sentence.

Did some return home? Well, some — just a few.
Most had no chance at all once their sentence was through.
The 'ticket-of-leave' was a chance to make good,
Some brave ones succeeded it's now understood.

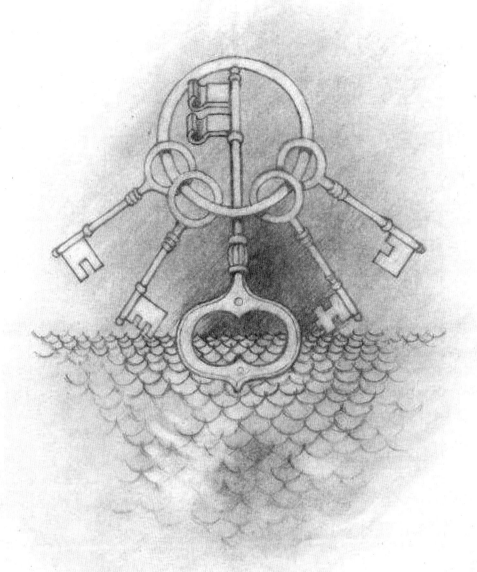

GLOSSARY

ANTIPODES	Opposite side of the world
BAILED UP	Held up by robbers
BEAK	Magistrate — slang term
BELAY	Tie off a rope
BIDDY	Woman — derogatory term
BILGE	Drain on a ship
BLOOMS	Flowers
BOSUN	Ship's officer
BOW STREET DOCK	Court house
BOW STREET RUNNERS	Police
BRACE OF PISTOLS	Two hand guns
BUMPKIN	Farm hand
CANVAS	Ships sails
CLOBBER	Clothing
CLOGS	Wooden shoes
COIN	Money
COBBLESTONES	Paving stones
COPSE	Clump of trees
DANDIES	Men of fashion
DOXY	Woman — derogatory term
ENLISTMENT SHILLING	Money given to men joining the Marines
FELONS	Convicts
FERAL	Untamed — dangerous person

FETTERS	Leg irons
FLASHY TOGS	Posh clothes
FLESH-POTS	Taverns — inns
FOBS	Ornaments on watch-chains
FOOTMAN	Servant
FOOTPAD	Robber on foot
GROG	Rum — alcoholic drink
GANGPLANK	Access on to a ship
HALF A CROWN	Twenty-five cents — money
HAMMOCK	Seaman's bed
HAVANAS	Cigars
HEATH	Grassy hillside
HIGHWAYMAN	Road-side robber — mounted
HOI-POLLOI	Local people — rough
HUNTERS	Pocket watches
JACK-TAR	Sailor
KNICK-KNACKS	Dressing table items
LOOT	Things stolen
LOBSTER	Royal Marine — joking term
LUBBER	From 'land lubber' not a seaman
MARINES	Soldiers who serve on ships
MASTS AND SPARS	Ship's poles and cross bars
MIND YOUR MANNERS	Very posh
NAUGHT	Nothing
NOWT	Nothing
NEWGATE	Notorious English prison
OLD-TUB	Ship — derogatory term
PENNIES	Cents — money
PAISLEY SHAWL	Scottish woven wrap

GLOSSARY

PIG-TAILS	Sailor's hair tied in pony-tail
PISTOLS PRIMED	Guns loaded
POACHING	Stealing game on private land
PRISON BARQUE	Prison ship
QUILL	Writing pen made from a feather
QUAFF	Drink
RAT-LINES	Rope ladders on a ship
RED-COATS	Soldiers
RIGGING	Ropes and sails on a ship
SHANTIES	Sailor's songs
SHILLING	Ten cents — money
SLUICE	Wash out
SMOCK	Farmer's work garment
SPRAY	Small bunch of flowers
STOCK	Neck tie — fabric or leather.
SWABBING DECKS	Washing down decks
SQUARE-RIGGED	Square sails on a ships
TANNER	Five-cent piece — money
TARS	Sailors
TART	Girl — derogatory term
TRAPS	Watchmen police
VALET	Gentleman's personal servant
VICTUALS	Stores — foodstuff
YARD ARM	Cross-bar on a mast
YOKEL	Country person — derogatory term
WAR-TIME TACK	Munitions — stores — uniforms
WENCH	Woman — country term
WIG	Magistrate — derogatory term

BRIAN HARRISON-LEVER

After an early career in television and film, Brian Harrison-Lever lectured in design and drawing at the Western Australian Academy of Performing Arts. His first picture book, 'In Flanders Fields', won the Children's Book Council of Australia's Picture Book of the Year in 2003, and the American ASPCA Henry Bergh Award in 2004. It was also short-listed for several state premiers' awards.

Two follow-up books, 'Photographs in the Mud', published in Australia and Japan, and 'The Call of the Osprey', have both won critical acclaim.

In 2007, with 'Three Kings', Harrison-Lever took on the dual role of author and illustrator. It received a Notable Book commendation from the Children's Book Council of Australia and was short-listed for the Western Australian State Premier's Award. His most recent illustration project was a retelling of Miles Franklin's 'My Brilliant Career'.

After many happy years living in the hills close to Perth on Australia's sunny west coast, Brian Harrison-Lever retired from academic life and moved with his wife Helen to Australia's beautiful southern island state, Tasmania.

OTHER BOOKS ILLUSTRATED BY BRIAN HARRISON-LEVER

'In Flanders Fields' (2002)   Written by Norman Jorgensen

'The Call of the Osprey' (2004)   Written by Norman Jorgensen

'Photographs in the Mud' (2005)   Written by Dianne Woolfer

'My Grandad Knew Phar Lap' (2006)   Written by Errol Broome

'Three Kings' (2007)   Written by Brian Harrison-Lever

'Castaway Convict' (2013)   Written by Wendy McDonald

'My Brilliant Career' (2014)   Written by Miles Franklin

Design by Brian Harrison-Lever
Layout by Kent Whitmore

Published by
Forty South Publishing Pty Ltd, Hobart, Tasmania
www.fortysouth.com.au

Printed by Choice Printing Group
www.choiceprintgroup.com